All the king's horses and all the king's men
Couldn't put **Humpty** together again!

The Owl and the **Pussycat** went to sea

by Edward Lear

HONEY

In a beautiful pea-green boat,
They took some honey, and plenty of money,
Wrapped up in a five-pound note.

The **Owl** looked up to the stars above,
And sang to a small guitar,
'O lovely Pussy! O Pussy, my love,
What a beautiful Pussy you are.'

One for my master,
One for my dame,
And one for the **little** boy
Who lives down the lane.

Twinkle, twinkle, little star, how I wonder what you are.

Up above the world so high, like a diamond in the sky.

Twinkle, twinkle little star, how I wonder what you are.

Hey diddle diddle,
The cat and the **fiddle**,
The cow jumped over the moon.